A LITTLE SPOT OF FEELINGS

OF FEELINGS

Written & Illustrated by Diane Alber

EMOTION DETECTIVE

To my children, Ryan and Anna

All inquiries about this book can be sent to the author at
info@dianealber.com
Published in the United States by Diane Alber Art LLC
ISBN 978-1-951287-40-5
For more information, or to book an event, visit our website:
www.dianealber.com
Hardcover
Printed in China

This book belongs to:

_____

_____

_____

Hi! My name is Scribble SPOT and I am a little SPOT of FEELINGS!

I'm so good at SPOTTING and NAMING FEELINGS, I actually became an EMOTION DETECTIVE.

It all started when I was tangled with EMOTIONS.
I didn't know how I was FEELING...

So I spent a lot of time learning all about EMOTIONS!
I learned that EMOTION SPOTS can show up for many reasons.
They can show up to help you, when people say and do things,
and when things happen around you.

Then these EMOTIONS start to create FEELINGS.

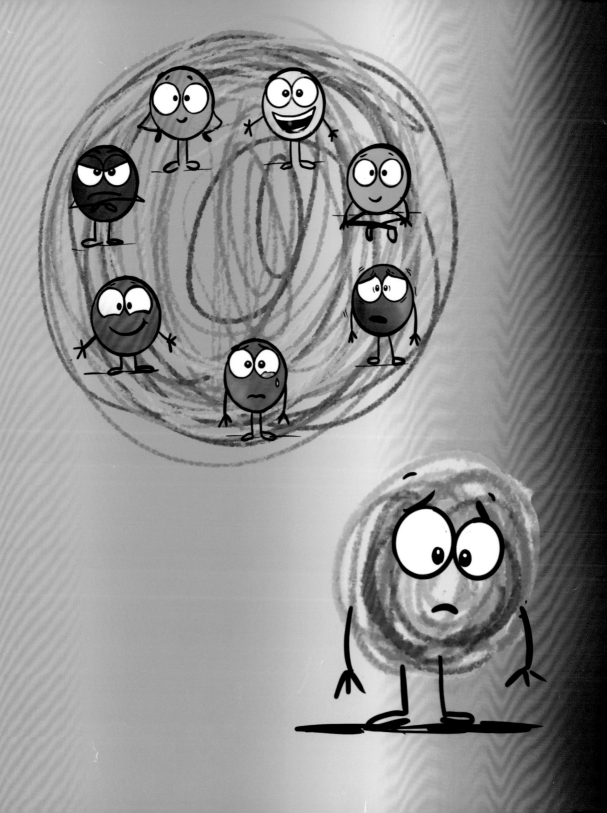

FEELINGS are very important, but when you don't know how you are FEELING it can be hard to explain what you need or how someone can help you.

Sometimes an EMOTION can create too many FEELINGS and they can get jumbled together.

So I made these FEELINGS CARDS to help you NAME your FEELINGS!

When you learn how to NAME your FEELINGS, it will help you get along with other people better and solve problems.

Then you will be on your way to becoming an EMOTION DETECTIVE like me!

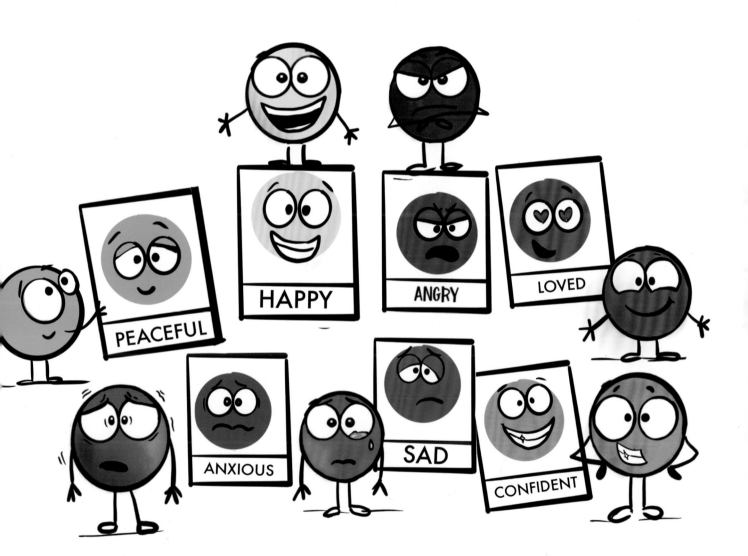

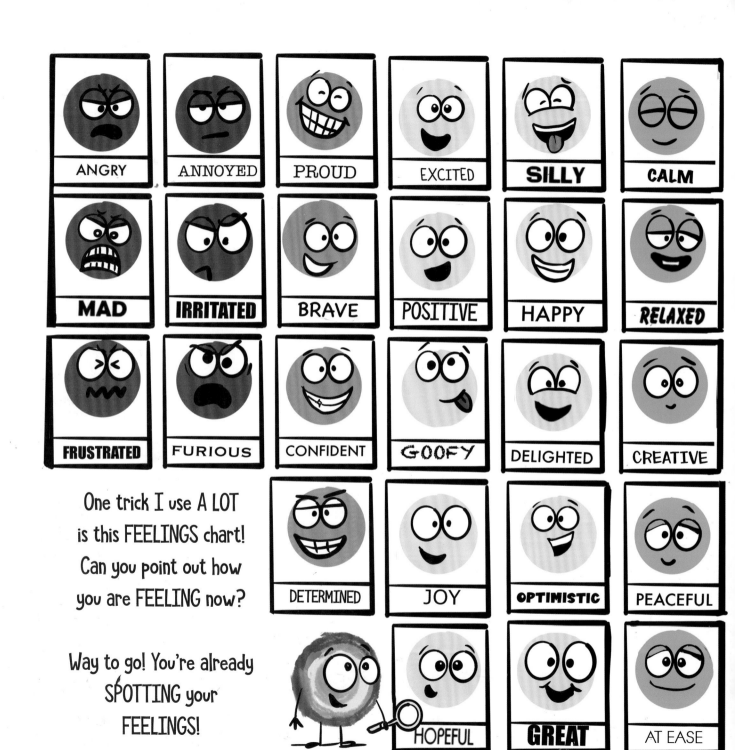

ANGRY

ANNOYED

PROUD

EXCITED

SILLY

CALM

MAD

IRRITATED

BRAVE

POSITIVE

HAPPY

RELAXED

FRUSTRATED

FURIOUS

CONFIDENT

GOOFY

DELIGHTED

CREATIVE

One trick I use A LOT
is this FEELINGS chart!
Can you point out how
you are FEELING now?

Way to go! You're already
SPOTTING your
FEELINGS!

DETERMINED

JOY

OPTIMISTIC

PEACEFUL

HOPEFUL

GREAT

AT EASE

 DISAPPOINTED

 **UPSET**

 ANXIOUS

 AFRAID

 SHY

 LOVED

 MISERABLE

 SAD

 UNEASY

 EMBARRASSED

 SCARED

 SPECIAL

 **HURT**

 LONELY

 WORRIED

 NERVOUS

 CONCERNED

 CARED FOR

 LEFT OUT

 DOWN

 FEAR

 **LOST**

 STRESSED

 APPRECIATED

 **DEFEATED**

 DISCOURAGED

 UNCOMFORTABLE

 *OVERWHELMED*

 INVISIBLE

CONFUSED

Another trick I like to use when SPOTTING FEELINGS is to look at FACE movements. Use a mirror to look closely at your EYEBROWS, EYES, and MOUTH, you will see how they move when you show your FEELINGS.

These movements are called FACIAL EXPRESSIONS. FACIAL EXPRESSIONS are CLUES to SPOTTING FEELINGS.

EYEBROWS

EYES

MOUTH

NAME IT!

Other CLUES are the way your BODY MOVES and how you stand. This is called BODY LANGUAGE.

BODY LANGUAGE

VOICE TONE
and VOLUME
are CLUES too!

AHHHHH!

SOUNDS

Now use these CLUES to SPOT your FEELING and NAME IT!

Let's look at a PEACEFUL SPOT. When it shows up, it can make you feel RELAXED and CALM.

PEACEFUL CLUES ARE:

- Relaxed eyebrows
- Focused and learning eyes
- Soft voice and breathing
- Ready to learn

PEACEFUL

Once you "NAME it," the final step is to "SAY it," and give a reason why! Start with, "I FEEL....when..."

This is your HAPPINESS SPOT. When it shows up, it can make you feel EXCITED and DELIGHTED.

HAPPINESS CLUES ARE:

- Eyebrows raised
- Eyes are crinkling
- Mouth corners turned up and smiling

When do you feel HAPPY?

This is your LOVE SPOT. When it shows up, it can make you feel LOVED and APPRECIATED.

LOVE CLUES ARE:

- Eyebrows raised
- Mouth turned upward smiling
- Wrinkled eyes
- Blushing and rosy cheeks

When do you feel LOVE?

This is your ANXIETY SPOT. When it shows up, it can make you feel SCARED or NERVOUS.

ANXIETY CLUES ARE:

- Eyebrows are turned up and wrinkled
- Head and eyes look down
- Slouching and not smiling
- Sweating and tummy ache

This is your SADNESS SPOT. When it shows up, it can make you feel SAD or LEFT OUT.

SADNESS CLUES ARE:

- Eyebrows turned up
- Watery eyes or crying
- Mouth turned down
- Hands covering face

When do you feel SAD?

This is your ANGER SPOT. When it shows up, it can make you feel FRUSTRATED or IRRITATED.

ANGER CLUES ARE:

- Eyebrows are lowered or turned down
- Eyes are very focused
- Mouth is frowning
- Strong voice and arms crossed

This is your CONFIDENCE SPOT. When it shows up,
it can make you feel PROUD and BRAVE.

CONFIDENT CLUES ARE:

- Eyebrows are relaxed
- Good eye contact
- Mouth corners turned up and smiling
- Strong voice

When do you
feel CONFIDENT?

Once you learn how to NAME your FEELINGS, you will discover new things about yourself.

It will also make you FEEL AMAZING!

Did you know that being able to SPOT your own FEELINGS helps you SPOT them in others?

What FEELING is everyone experiencing here?

So...are you ready to start training to be an
EMOTION DETECTIVE?

Beyond the book reading and activities:

This book is a great way to start conversations about FEELINGS with your child. Go to the FEELINGS chart in this book, have your child pick a random FEELING and create the FACIAL EXPRESSION. Using a mirror will help your child see what face movements they are making. Ask your child when they felt that FEELING. Talk about when you felt that feeling.

From the Author:

Thank you so much for taking the time to read this book! This story was developed to help children recognize FEELINGS, not only in themselves but in others . They do this by learning FACIAL EXPRESSIONS and BODY LANGUAGE. Identifying and naming your EMOTIONS is the first step in managing your FEELINGS. For coping and managing techniques, I created a companion series that breaks out each EMOTION individually to highlight specific examples and strategies that are easy to understand and apply to everyday life!

Diane Alber

For free printables and worksheets that go along with these books, visit www.dianealber.com